OSCEOLA'S HEAD

Prentice-Hall, Inc., Englewood Cliffs, N.J.

OSCEOLA'S HEAD

and Other American Ghost Stories

by Walter Harter

illustrated by Neil Waldman

10   9   8   7   6   5   4   3   2   1
Copyright © 1974 by   Walter L. Harter

Printed in the United States of America • J

Prentice-Hall International, Inc., London
Prentice-Hall of Australia, Pty. Ltd., North Sydney
Prentice-Hall of Canada, Ltd., Toronto
Prentice-Hall of India Private Ltd., New Delhi
Prentice-Hall of Japan, Inc., Tokyo

This book is set in 14/16 TIMES ROMAN
by P & M Typesetting, Inc.

Book design by Dann Jacobus

Library of Congress Cataloging in Publication Data

Harter, Walter L
  Osceola's head and other American ghost stories.

  SUMMARY: Ten stories present the historical
backgrounds of ghosts still haunting Valley Forge,
the White House, and other places throughout the
United States.
  1. Ghost stories. [1.   Ghost stories. 2.   United
States—History—Fiction]   I.   Waldman, Neil, illus.
II. Title.
PZ7.H260s   [Fic]   73–13892
ISBN 0–13–642991–2

To Edna
who believes in those things
that make strange noises in the night

TABLE OF CONTENTS

INTRODUCTION

There are many different kinds of ghosts. Some are seen. Some are felt. Some are only heard. Ghosts are usually floating, white-clad, transparent figures that pass easily through walls and doors. They appear instantly, and disappear just as quickly.

Not all ghosts are dressed in white, though. Many of them are arrayed in the clothes of the times in which they lived. Ghostly knights wear armor. Ghostly Indians wear buckskins and feathers. Ghosts are also called wraiths, apparitions and phantoms, among other things.

Ghosts almost always take a human shape. Many appear to be the figures of relatives who have died. Very often these ancestors had violent deaths, and were not ready to leave this life. Therefore they return, either to deliver messages to their loved ones, or to complete plans that had been interrupted by their sudden deaths. Sometimes they return to give warnings of coming events, usually unpleasant. Or they might return to seek revenge. It is said that when ghosts finish the work they left behind, or have brought justice to their enemies, they have found peace, and are seen no more. Then there are ghosts that return again and again to certain places, for no apparent reasons. Except, perhaps, that they liked those places when they were alive.

Ghosts can also be the spirits of anything that once was alive. There are stories of pets, especially dogs, cats, and horses that were so loved by their masters that they returned after death to keep them company.

Ghosts that have appeared in the same places for many years are unfamiliar to those who see them now. They are historical ghosts, and they can be more frightening than the ghosts of relatives or friends. For most of us fear the unknown and the strange.

A knight who was killed by a rival in a contest to win the hand of a beautiful maiden, might still haunt that field of battle, even though now it is a busy city street. The two Indians in a story in this book, "The Ghosts of Foley Square," might be frightening when seen now. But they were familiar figures to their fellow tribesmen hundreds of years ago.

Therefore no ghosts should be feared. For if we knew their stories we would understand why they return to the places they knew in life. And when we understand we don't fear.

Some ghosts that aren't seen, but only heard, are called poltergeists. This is a combination of two German words—*polter*, meaning uproar or disturbance, and *geist*, meaning spirit or ghost. When a poltergeist takes possession of a house it can make life miserable for the occupants by slamming doors, breaking dishes, turning lights on and off, and doing many more annoying things.

Very often, of course, there are reasonable explanations for these disturbances. A sudden draft can make a door slam. A dish that has been carelessly placed on a shelf can fall and break. But often, too, there are no reasonable explanations. Sometimes poltergeists can be persuaded to vacate the premises if the live occupants of the house march through the halls and rooms, banging loudly on pots and pans and sternly ordering the pests to "Go away!" In some countries there are people who make a profession of ridding homes of these annoying visitors. But most people, when they realize a poltergeist has become part of their family, try to get used to the irritating tricks, or they move.

Ghosts that are only *felt* can be disturbing too. You might be sitting reading, or strolling down the

3

street, and suddenly shiver with cold. That could mean that a ghost is passing by, or that one is walking or sitting beside you. There is no harm in these chilly visitors, and the only solution is to button your jacket tighter, or put on a sweater.

Witches are of many kinds too. They are thought of as being mostly women, but some are men, and these are called Warlocks. For a long time witches were thought of as old, scrawny women, who walked with gnarled canes or rode broomsticks through the air. But witches can look like ordinary people, even young and pretty children. Witches can cast "spells," that make normal people do good or bad things. Although most of them are thought to have some arrangement with the Devil, many are good witches, who try to undo evil spells.

Many learned people do not believe these strange things exist. They say they are only in the imagination. They even claim there are reasonable answers to why the writings on some walls are impossible to erase, or why handprints in some places return fresh and clear even after the stones or walls on which they first appeared have been replaced.

But just as many intelligent persons do believe, and have believed, that there are many mysteries in our world and in the air around us that have never been explained. Franklin Delano Roosevelt was one of the people who believed, and so was Abraham Lincoln. George Washington saw several ghosts during his lifetime. One of them, described in this book, visited him during that terrible winter at Valley Forge and inspired him to continue fighting the Revolutionary War.

Even the White House in Washington, D.C. is the home of some famous ghosts. Sometimes if a tourist wanders into the lovely rose garden there and picks a few blooms, it is said that a small, pretty woman rushes out of a side door and orders that person away. It is the spirit of Dolley Madison, wife of the fourth President of the United States, who planted the first rose bush in that spot more than 150 years ago.

Then there is the tale of the small boy who wandered away from a group of visitors being guided through the many public rooms of the White House. He became lost and frightened. Then, he told his parents later, a tall man wearing a beard, took him by the hand and gave him a personal tour of the private rooms. In one of them, known as "The Lincoln Room," the bearded man told the boy, "This was my room."

Ghosts have been seen, and are being seen, on lonely farms in our midwest, in the bright sunlight of Florida and California, and in busy cities like New York, Boston and Chicago. They all have a reason for being where they are and doing what they do. There is space in this book to describe only a few of them.

Neil Waldman

THE GHOST AT VALLEY FORGE

Late in the afternoon of a bitterly cold day in December 1777, General George Washington stood at a window of a small house close to the village of Valley Forge, in southeastern Pennsylvania. He was watching his small army of weary and half-starved soldiers plod with bloody feet onto the bleak and barren ground that would be their winter quarters.

Colonel Newhouse, who stood beside that same window watching the men toil through the snow drifts, wrote to his wife: "You could track our army from Philadelphia to Valley Forge by the blood dripping from their feet." In that same letter he added, "For three days we have been without food. The men must have meat or they will no longer be able to stand."

They had marched twenty miles from their

previous lines at Whitemarsh, near Philadelphia. It had taken the exhausted men two days—two days during which it had snowed almost constantly.

Some people called it a retreat, and perhaps it was. But the British army, with General Howe at its head, had also withdrawn from the field of battle. However, the British soldiers would be stationed in warm houses in Philadelphia, with plenty of food, where they could repair or renew their equipment, and prepare for new battles in the spring.

The American soldiers had neither food nor shelter, and the little equipment they possessed was almost beyond repair. The Continental Congress had no money to spend on new arms, even if any were available.

General Washington had led his army to Valley Forge for the winter so they would be safe from attacks by the British in Philadelphia. He knew his soldiers could not travel any further. Their strength was gone. This might, he told Colonel Newhouse, be the end of the Revolutionary War. The behavior of the soldiers was remarkable. Earlier Washington had written to his wife: "I'm surprised that our famished troops have not been driven to widespread desertion, mutiny, or pillage." But the soldiers did not revolt, and very few deserted. However, their officers, especially General Washington, had to face the facts. There were few arms and no food, and no money to buy either.

8

General Washington had to make an important decision. If he disbanded the army and allowed the weary men to go home, the War of Independence might be over. For months the British army had been gaining strength. Every fleet of ships that entered the harbors of Philadelphia and New York brought fresh men and materials. If the Continental soldiers spent the bitter winter at Valley Forge many might die from cold and starvation. In the spring, those that survived would easily be conquered by the stronger British troops.

George Washington and his officers did all they could to help their men during the long hours of that first terrible night. They helped build fires and cover the wounded with straw. There was little else they could do except huddle by the fires and wait for dawn.

After midnight General Washington, unable to sleep, walked to the brow of a small hill that overlooked the winking fires of his army. "I sensed a presence near me," he wrote to a friend. "A man, not a soldier, and one whom I had never seen before, approached me. He was tall and bareheaded, and wore a coat that fell to his boots. He pointed down the hill, away from the camp. I saw, as if by a miracle, not one but many large cities. Each one, to my agitated mind, seemed more populous than our whole country. The people were busy and happy. I passed my hand over my eyes to clear the dream, if it was a dream, and turned to the person beside me. But he was gone. However he *had* been there, and I *did* see those cities."

The next morning General Washington issued orders that meant the difference between defeat and the eventual winning of the war.

Those soldiers who knew how to handle axes, saws, and hammers, were to begin building cabins, each one to hold twelve men. Washington offered a reward of twelve dollars for the first cabin to be constructed in each regiment. There was plenty of wood and the work progressed rapidly.

Other soldiers were sent into the countryside to forage for food. But they could not, according to Washington's orders, rob the inhabitants of horses, cattle, or grain. They were to pay for each item with promisory notes bearing General Washington's own signature as assurance that they would eventually be paid.

In a few weeks a thousand cabins lined carefully laid out paths on the frozen ground at Valley Forge. Although there never was enough food, the men were fed. Cloth was distributed among the women in farmhouses as distant as Lancaster, where it was quickly made into pants and shirts for the needy soldiers.

Slowly the long winter months passed, each one bringing some improvement to the men. By springtime it was a much stronger army than the one that had stumbled through the snow to Valley Forge on that cold December day—an army that struggled on to win the War of Independence.

General Washington often spoke of the vision he'd had that first night at Valley Forge, and of the "apparition," as he called it, that had stood beside him. On one occasion when Colonel Laurens, an old war friend, was visiting him at Mount Vernon, Washington said, "I must have been delirious that night . . . but . . . I'm *never* delirious."

Neil Waldman

BLOODY HANDPRINTS ON THE WALL

Deep within the Navajo Indian Reservation, in the state of Utah, there's a place called *Canon del Muerto*—Canyon of the Dead. It's a lonely place, barren of vegetation, and strewn with rocks and boulders. On very rare occasions it is visited by prospectors and archeologists, but very few Indians ever go there.

It is haunted.

In the simple hogans of the Navajos—houses built of adobe, wood, and mud—ancient chiefs tell tales of the ghosts that roam the rim of the canyon. They tell of screams that pierce the clear night air, but mostly they tell about the blood-stained hand-prints that are on the wall of a cave high in the side of the canyon. For it was in that cave, almost 175 years ago, that more than a hundred Navajo and

Pueblo Indians were massacred by Spaniards who rode up from Sante Fe, New Mexico, seeking revenge.

This is the story told by the old men of the tribes.

By the beginning of the 1600's Spaniards from Mexico had pushed north into what is now New Mexico. They built settlements and forts and hunted for gold and furs in the hunting grounds of the Indian tribes that lived in that area. The Pueblos were the largest and strongest of those tribes, and they fought many fierce battles with the Spaniards to protect their homes and hunting grounds. Eventually, however, the Spaniards with their guns and armor conquered most of the Pueblos and pushed them farther north into what is now the state of Utah.

The Pueblos and Navajos became friends and joined forces against the marauding Spaniards. The Pueblos taught their new friends how to dig cave-homes high in the cliffs of the canyons, and how to plant corn. Eventually small cities of caves clung to the sheer sides of the canyons, and below, on the plains, fields of corn waved their tassels in the constant wind that blew across the prairies.

But the Pueblos never forgot their old homes in the south, nor could they forget the many women and children who had died under the hoofs of the heavy Spanish horses when the conquistadors had trampled their homes into dust.

14

For many months the Pueblos and Navajos made plans to attack the Spanish settlements that had sprung up around Sante Fe. Some of the Indians had guns, taken from fallen Spaniards, but most had only bows and arrows. What they depended upon for success was their numbers. For the Spaniards were still relatively few, while the Indians were in the thousands.

Early in the spring of 1805 more than 500 Pueblos and Navajos on swift ponies began the long ride to Sante Fe. They reached the outlying settlements a week later.

Ten small Spanish garrisons were overrun. Each one consisted of a tiny fort and a few houses. Every Spaniard in each fort was killed, and the houses burned. After more than a week of killing the Indians turned north to Utah and their canyons.

Now it was the Spaniards' turn for revenge.

In the fall of 1805 part of a regiment of Spanish cavalry, under the command of Lt. Antonio Narbona, was sent to punish the Pueblos and Navajos.

Early one bright morning in October a Navajo lookout, perched on the rim of one of the canyons, saw a cloud of dust where the flat prairie met the horizon. It was dust raised by the hoofs of 400 huge Spanish horses.

The lookout spread the alarm immediately, and by the time the first Spaniards reined in their horses at the opening to the canyons those Indians

15

who hadn't mounted their ponies and sped away had climbed into the caves that honeycombed the high cliffs.

The Spaniards took their time. They attacked each cave separately, climbing ladders to the openings and firing into the masses of Indians. Those who tried to escape were flung screaming onto the rocks below.

Finally, by the end of that first day, all the Indians had been killed except those in one cave, the largest and highest that had been dug into the cliff of the canyon now known as *Canon del Muerto*.

The Indians in the last cave fought courageously. They barricaded the entrance with rocks and pieces of wood, leaving only a small space from which they could rush out and push away the ladders of the invaders.

At last the Spaniards decided to make camp on the floor of the canyon and starve the Indians into surrendering. At the end of ten days the Indians, crazed with fear and weak from lack of food and water, killed themselves. Fathers and sons flung mothers, wives and children onto the rocks below. The strongest men slew the weaker, and then they too jumped to their deaths.

Lt. Narbona cut off the ears of 84 dead Indians and delivered them to the Spanish governor at Sante Fe in proof of the success of the expedition.

When the Spaniards entered the cave they found dozens of bloody handprints in two rows across the rear wall. Apparently some of the Indians, made insane by fear and hunger, had slashed their palms and fingers and pressed them against the stone.

The ghostly handprints can still be seen on the wall of that cave in the *Canon del Muerto*. Souvenir hunters have tried to cut them from the wall, and scientists have attempted to remove them for display in museums. But even when the stones are taken down and replaced with new ones, the handprints return, as fresh as they were originally. And, according to the new Indians who venture near the *Canon del Muerto*, ghostly figures still roam the rim, and screams still pierce the still night air.

Neil Waldman

JAMIE DAWKIN'S DRUM

Paul Revere was more than an express rider who galloped toward Lexington on a dark and windy night in 1777 with news of the British landing at Boston. He was a master silversmith and knew how to protect the bottoms of the ships with copper for our small navy. He made cannons and huge church bells. He was a colonel in the Continental Army. And he was also partly responsible for the ghost of an English drummer boy who, some people say, still parades the streets of a small town in Maine.

By 1779 the Revolutionary War was being fought throughout the thirteen colonies. Sometimes the Americans had the advantage, at other times the British, with their hired Hessian soldiers, seemed to be winning. The eastern coast of the United States was like a giant chessboard, with moves and counter-moves by both sides.

One of the moves the British made was to place two regiments of soldiers and three heavily armed warships at the small village of Castine, in Maine (which was then a part of Massachusetts). Located on the coast of Penobscot Bay, Castine was on the route of American fishing boats carrying supplies up and down the coast to the Continental soldiers. The British planned to use Castine as a base in their attack on Boston and sink those small boats.

When the Continental Congress and General Washington found out about the British plan they decided to attack the British soldiers and ships at the small village. But that plan wasn't easy to put into operation because the army in the north, commanded by General Lovell, was mostly made up, in his words, of "small boys and old men unfit for service."

Most of the experienced Continental soldiers were with General Washington in the south, around New York and Philadelphia.

However, the threat to the Massachusetts fishing boats had to be stopped. Several regiments of Continental soldiers—one of them commanded by Colonel Paul Revere—were ordered to the village of Castine with instructions to attack the British by surprise and attempt to sink the warships.

The patriots were to go by sea, crammed aboard small fishing boats, and any other vessels that were available. It was a difficult task to make all the necessary arrangements. Food had to be brought on board, and a few cannons—three nine-pounders and four field pieces—had to be lashed to the decks of two of the larger boats.

After a slow three day voyage the dozen or so small boats arrived at the opening of Penobscot Bay. There they anchored and held a council to make plans. For an entire day and night the officers argued about what to do. Revere and several others wanted to advance boldly into the bay and land the soldiers for a ground attack. After nightfall smaller boats, equipped with bombs, would be sent against the warships. They were certain that once the small boats got close enough so that large guns couldn't be brought to bear on them, they could attach the bombs to the bottom of the warships and sink them.

After much arguing that plan was agreed to, and by late afternoon of the following day the fishing boats began to enter the bay.

But they had argued and waited too long.

After all the fishing boats had entered the bay and it was still daylight, lookouts were astonished to see four more British warships approaching from the sea. General McLein, commander of the British units at Castine, had sent to Lord Howe at New York for reinforcements. The guns of the warships inside the bay and those coming in from the sea began firing as soon as they saw the American boats.

The Continental soldiers, most of them inexperienced in warfare, panicked. They ran their small boats ashore and, dropping rifles and food, fled through the forests toward Boston.

Night fell. British regiments at Castine and their comrades who arrived on warships pursued the fleeing Americans through the streets of the village. At times some American soldiers stopped running and tried to fight a delaying action. Paul Revere tried his best to rally the men and form some kind of line of battle, but it was useless.

The fighting raged through the narrow streets of the village, while both Americans and British fired wildly into the night. Finally the last American disappeared toward Boston and the English soldiers returned to their ships.

Many American officers were punished because of that defeat. Paul Revere was relieved of his command, but he insisted on a court-martial. After the officers heard the testimony of the men who fought with him that night, he was proved to be innocent of the charges of cowardice and disobedience, and given an honorable discharge from the Continental Army.

With all the shooting that went on during that wild night of confusion at Penobscot Bay, there was only one death. Jamie Dawkins, a twelve year old drummer boy (son of one of the British soldiers) was killed by a richocheting bullet.

At dawn the next morning his body was found, the small leather drum still strapped to his shoulders, and his fingers still clutching the drumsticks. The American inhabitants of Castine and the British garrison joined in giving the boy a full military funeral. He was buried in the local cemetery.

Castine is still a small village on the shores of Penobscot Bay. When the wind is from the east, and there is a stillness in the air, especially during those calm hours just before dawn, there sometimes can be heard the faint rat-a-tat-tat of a drum. And some people have sometimes seen a small boy, dressed in a British uniform, marching through the quiet streets.

Neil Waldman

OSCEOLA'S HEAD

Almost all the ghosts that are seen appear to be complete with arms, legs, a body and a head. But one historical apparition is different. It is *only* a head —a head bound in a colorful turban from which hang three wild turkey feathers.

The story began in Florida, at noon of a balmy day in October, 1837. In a small clearing beside a creek, near the present city of Ocala, a group of Seminole chiefs stood quietly waiting. Each Indian had a small square of white cotton cloth tied to the barrel of his rifle.

In the center of the group of chiefs stood Osceola, their leader. He was a tall man. His complexion was lighter than the others because he was only half Indian. His father had been an English trader named Powell. His mother was a Creek.

Osceola was noticeable not only because he was taller and lighter than the others, but also because of his colorful clothes. His hunting shirt was bright blue. His leather leggings had been dyed red. On his head was a turban made of red and white striped cloth. From it hung three long feathers that had been dyed white, red, and blue.

Osceola glanced at the sky. The sun was directly overhead. It was exactly noon. At that instant a group of American soldiers, led by Lieutenant General Hernandez, galloped out of a forest of palm trees and came to a halt in front of the Seminoles. For a few seconds the Indians and white soldiers stared at one another. Then General Hernandez ordered, "Seize them!"

And so began one of the most shameful acts of the U.S. Government against the Indians of Florida.

The Seminole chiefs had gathered trustfully under the white flags of truce. The white squares had been sent to them by Major General Jessup, commander of the U.S. forces in northern Florida, with the promise that the chiefs would be safe if they carried the flags and met with him to discuss peace.

In 1821 the United States had acquired the Territory of Florida from Spain. There were, of course, many difficulties in administering that wild land. It had been ruled twice by Spain and once by England. Each nation had so defrauded and persecuted the Indians that finally the Seminoles had come to hate all white men.

For many years the Indians had attacked outlying settlements in northern Florida, trying to regain some of the rich land that had been taken from them. But worst of all, in the eyes of the white men, the Seminoles protected the slaves that ran away from their masters in Georgia and fled for safety in the Florida swamps.

Finally the United States decided that all the Seminoles should be taken from Florida and sent west to Oklahoma territory. In an agreement made at Moultrie Creek it was agreed by some of the Indian chiefs that the Seminoles of northern Florida would leave their homeland within a year.

But Osceola and many other chiefs didn't agree. The treaty demanded that all runaway slaves must be given up. This Osceola refused to do. He and other chiefs also claimed that, because they hadn't signed the agreement, it wasn't binding on them or their followers.

General Jessup decided that the only way to make sure that all the Indians would comply to the treaty was to capture Osceola and his friends. If *they* were taken by force to the western lands the other Indians might follow.

After Osceola and the other defiant chiefs were captured under the flags of truce that October day, they were marched to St. Augustine and thrown in the dungeons of the old fort, Castillo de San Marcos.

The chiefs were kept there for several weeks. However when an outbreak of yellow fever occurred they were taken by ship to Fort Marion in South Carolina and placed in cells.

It was there that Osceola died.

Some say he had caught the yellow fever before leaving St. Augustine, and finally succumbed to it. But others who were with him at Fort Marion, both white men and Indians, were sure he died of a broken heart. The night he died he carefully dressed himself in his best garments, complete with turban and feathers, and passed among those who were with him in the cells, wishing them well and thanking them for their services. Then he calmly lay down and passed away. He was buried in a shallow grave close to the fort.

Many years later, after Florida had become the 27th state of the Union, it was decided that Osceola should be reburied in the land where he had been born, in the earth he had fought so desperately to defend.

However when his grave was opened it was discovered that the body was there—but the head had disappeared.

Dr. Frederick Weedon, who had accompanied Osceola to Fort Marion, and who was with the Indian leader when he died, confessed that he had taken Osceola's head back with him to his home in St. Augustine. The famous head was said to have passed through many hands during the following years, and finally was placed in the Surgical and Pathological Museum in the University of the City of New York. In 1866 a great fire swept through the museum and many specimens were lost. Osceola's head was said to have been among them.

The old fort of Castillo de San Marcos in St. Augustine is thronged with visitors every day. They peer into the dungeons and take pictures of one another on the wide battlements. But at sundown each day, when the flag is lowered, and the tourists depart, the old fort sinks into quietness.

However, many tourists who stroll around the deep moats after dark and glance up at the high walls that are often bathed in moonlight, stop and stare. Many have claimed that they see a head wrapped in a turban of many colors, with three long feathers hanging from it.

The head always seems to rest, or float, directly over the dungeon where the defiant Indian leader was kept in chains.

From descriptions of the turban, feathers, and especially the features, many think it's the head of Osceola, returning again and again.

But whatever else the floating head means, it's a symbol of courage to the Seminoles. For they are the only American Indians who have never signed a peace treaty with the United States.

Neil Waldman

THE HOUSE THAT
HATED WAR

    It isn't often that more than two or three ghosts are seen at one time. But there *is* one place in the United States where sometimes dozens and hundreds of spirits appear together.

    It all began early on a bright Sunday morning, April 9, 1865, when three men in the grey uniforms of the Confederate cavalry, galloped into the tiny village of Appomattox Court House, in northern Virginia.

    The leader of the riders, Colonel Charles Marshall, had been ordered by General Robert E. Lee "to find a suitable place where I can meet with General Grant and surrender my army to him."

    By early April, 1865, the men of the last great fighting force of the South were completely surrounded by Union soldiers. They had no food, and very little ammunition. Although the spirit of those brave Southerners was high, and they would have preferred to fight on, their situation was hopeless. "I would rather die a thousand deaths than do this," General Lee told one of his aides, "But I don't want one more man to die."

Two days earlier General Grant had sent a message to the southern general, suggesting that lives would be saved if the South were to surrender at once. General Lee had asked for two days to think it over. That time was now up. And he had made his decision. Lee sent a message to General Grant, asking that they meet to discuss terms.

Colonel Marshall examined several houses in the village, but none of them were large enough to accommodate the number of officers who would attend the momentous meeting.

Then, in the dusty square of the town, he met a man whose name has been entered in the history of that stirring time. Not only because it was his house that was selected for the meeting, but also because of the strange circumstances that brought him to the village.

The man's name was Wilmer McLean. He was a farmer. He also hated war. Four years before, in 1861, he had lived in another village in Virginia. It was called Manassas. Near it flowed a small creek with the strange name of Bull Run.

It was there, at Bull Run, that one of the first great battles of the Civil War was fought. Mr. Mc-Lean's land was covered with the bodies of the dead and dying. To escape from that terrible picture of men, sometimes brothers, killing one another, he moved his family farther South. It was in that little village, on the bright Sunday morning, that he offered his house as a setting for the meeting that would end a horrible and long war.

A few hours after Colonel Marshall talked with Mr. McLean, a tall, grey-haired man accompanied by some officers, rode down the dirt road to the house that sat near fields of waving corn. He was General Robert E. Lee.

He was dressed in a new uniform of grey. By his side swung a sword decorated in gold. He slowly dismounted from his white horse, Traveler, the animal that had carried him through four years of death and destruction, and entered the parlor of the house that hated war. There General Lee ordered Colonel Marshall "to put a man on the road so that General Grant will know where we are."

Half an hour later a group of riders dressed in dusty blue uniforms came to a clattering halt in front of the McLean house.

They made a striking contrast with the men awaiting them. The Confederate officers had dressed in their best for the occasion. The Union officers, including General Grant, were in their field uniforms, dirty and wrinkled from hours in the saddle.

The small, dark General Grant and the tall, elegant General Lee shook hands, and immediately got down to business. The terms offered by Grant were generous. Each southern officer could keep his side-arms, and a horse, if one were available. Food was to be sent immediately to the hungry men.

In an hour it was over. General Grant and his officers, although the last to arrive, left first. Then slowly the defeated southern officers mounted their horses and rode away. The last to leave was the tall man on the white horse. Finally Mr. McLean stood alone in the parlor of his house.

But never again was that house ever really alone.

Three days after the meeting between Generals Lee and Grant, the formal surrender took place. Early on the morning of April 12, 1865, the Union soldiers formed two long lines on the dusty road that led from the village to the Confederate encampment.

To the sounds of a military band the vanquished southern soldiers marched briskly between the lanes of blue and deposited their guns and ammunition in an open field. As they passed through the ranks of Union men both armies raised their hands in a salute to their former foes.

After the weapons had been gathered, an officer read General Lee's message of thanks and farewell to his defeated soldiers. Then the men were dismissed, and began the long walk to their homes in various parts of the south. However one Confederate soldier, Charles F. Sweeney, had only to walk across the road to reach his house and waiting family.

The McLean family continued to live in the house for the next four years. Then a group of businessmen thought it would be a profitable idea to buy the house, dismantle it, and take it to Washington, D.C. There it would be reassembled and an admission charged to view the famous room.

The house *was* taken apart, and piled on a corner of the property. And there it lay, *abandoned by the living*, for more than eighty years.

But the spirits of the men who had met there on that Sunday, April 9, 1865, didn't forget.

One by one, as those officers in grey and blue passed away, their ghosts wandered back to that spot where the most momentous event in their lives had taken place.

The rumors began only a few years after the McLean house became a pile of rubble. At first only one, then two, then three phantoms were seen, their forms transparent in the midday sun. And voices were heard, sometimes during the day, but more often at night. Some young farm lads on their way home from courting local girls, claimed they often were stopped as they hurried along that dusty road by soldiers in blue and in grey, who asked them to give the "password" of the day.

As the years passed, and as others who had participated on that great occasion finally died, more men in grey and blue—some on horseback and some on foot—were seen around the area. The spirits seemed to be searching for something.

Finally in 1930 the United States Government bought what was left of the McLean house and various other pieces of property at Appomattox. The plan was to reconstruct the small village exactly as it had been on that bright Sunday morning so long ago. The work progressed slowly. There were many interruptions. World War II was one of them. However at last, in 1949, the last nail was driven into the wooden beams of the McLean house.

Now other men in uniforms are in charge of the room where the two greatest generals of the Civil War met to put a stop to senseless killing. They are employees of the National Park Service, who guide visitors through various buildings of the village, and especially through the most famous house of all. At night the buildings are closed and the uniformed men go home to their families. But the McLean house is never empty.

Some people who have gone there at night say

they hear the voices of many men, and the sound of booted footsteps and the ring of iron spurs on the wood floor.

On some moonlit nights a tall man in a grey uniform, astride a white horse, has been seen to ride slowly away from the house. The man and horse turn into a dusty road and disappear in the direction where, more than a hundred years ago, a mighty army of soldiers in grey huddled around their camp-fires.

It isn't at all strange that the spirits of these men in grey and blue return to that place.

For it was in that area, in that house, in that room, where a broken nation was made whole again.

THE ACTOR WHO WON'T STAY DEAD

Ford's Theater in Washington, D.C., is one of the most modern playhouses in the United States. It was rebuilt and restored in 1968, almost on the ashes of the theater that stood on that site for more than a hundred years. The "new" theater is filled with the latest mechanical and electronic conveniences.

And yet, some of the actors and other people who are employed there claim the place is haunted.

Actors who are letter-perfect in their parts, who have played the same roles many times in other theaters, suddenly forget cues and lines when on stage at Ford's Theater.

These "accidents" always seem to happen when the actors are standing on an imaginary line that stretches from a flag-draped box on the right side of the stage *across* the stage to a doorway on the left. Also, many actors say, they often feel "chills" when they cross that line.

And in that box, where the American flags are draped over the railing, chairs are sometimes shuffled into bizarre patterns, and the pictures on the walls are either pulled from the nails holding them, or shifted to 45 degree angles.

Not only actors have felt the presence of this theatrical ghost. Workmen in the theater sometimes hear clumping footsteps, as though someone in heavy boots is walking or running through the corridors.

Who is this ghost? And why does he haunt Ford's Theater. Perhaps it began on a spring evening over a hundred years ago.

The evening of Tuesday, April 14, 1865, was warm and balmy. The dust on the dirt streets of Washington rose in tiny swirls as the horse-drawn carriages passed in front of Ford's Theater.

It was to be a gala night at the theater. Not only was Miss Laura Keene to give her last performance in the comedy, *Our American Cousin*, but President and Mrs. Lincoln were to attend.

Two special carriages were in the line of traffic that drew up in front of the brightly lighted entrance to the theater. From the first stepped a tall, bearded man wearing a dark cloak and tall hat. He turned and gently helped a small, portly woman to alight. Abraham Lincoln and his wife had arrived.

Six men ran from the second carriage and quickly surrounded the tall man and the small woman. They were men especially selected from the Union Army to protect the President and his family.

Even though Civil War hostilities had ceased, there were many Southerners who hated the President, and who had sworn to kill him. Therefore extreme precautions had been taken for his safety that night. Only the Presidential box would be occupied; the others would remain empty. Armed soldiers and secret agents would patrol the corridors.

The play began on time, and proceeded with professional smoothness. However, midway in the second act there was an interruption. Abraham Lincoln, sixteenth President of the United States, was murdered.

Shortly before ten o'clock that evening a man dressed in black, and wearing high riding boots, galloped to the stage door of the theater. He swung from the saddle, flung the reins to a waiting boy, and strode into the theater.

The man was known to the door-keeper and to the others he passed on his way across the back of the stage. He was John Wilkes Booth, age 27, a well-known actor and man-about-town.

Booth quickly mounted the steps to the corridor on the second floor, where doors opened into the boxes. He had planned his moves carefully, and knew exactly which door led to where the President would be sitting.

In one hand Booth carried a small pistol, in the other a knife. He expected to find a guard at the door and the knife was to be used to kill him quickly and silently. The pistol was to be used to murder the President.

But no one was on guard before the door.

Apparently the soldier had left his post to watch the performance. There were so many guards throughout the theater that he probably thought there was no danger for the President.

Booth quickly opened the door and slipped into the anteroom that led to the box. At the inner door he hesitated a moment, a gloved hand on the knob—then flung it open.

The President was sitting directly in front of him. Booth took two steps forward, pressed the pistol against the side of Lincoln's head, and pulled the trigger.

For a moment after the report there was silence. Then Mrs. Lincoln, who was seated a little in front of the President and to one side, saw what had happened, and screamed.

Booth ran to the edge of the box and leaped over it. But one of his spurs caught in the flag that was draped there, and he fell to the stage, His left leg doubled under him. It was broken. In a second he was up again, running, limping on the broken leg.

He crossed the stage, threatening with pistol

and knife anyone who tried to stop him. Outside the stagedoor he tore the reins from the waiting boy, flung himself into the saddle, and dashed away.

For twelve long days John Wilkes Booth was hunted as if he were a mad animal. On April 26 he finally was cornered in a barn in Virginia. There, exhausted and delirious with pain, he put the pistol to his head and killed himself.

Is it the ghost of John Wilkes Booth that haunts the stage and corridors of Ford's Theater?

No one has even seen the ghost, but many have felt his presence. The actors who forget their lines and feel the chill of death when they stand in the path the murderer took when he crossed the stage seem to think the spirit of the fiery actor still wanders there. And the workers who clean the box and find the chairs and pictures disturbed think so too.

The day after the assassination Matthew Brady, the famous Civil War photographer, made pictures of all parts of the interior of the theater. In one of the photographs there is the shadow of a strange figure standing next to the box Lincoln occupied that fateful night.

Perhaps it *is* a picture of the assassin, condemned for eternity to remain where he had committed his crime.

Those who hear the clumping of his boots in the corridors think so.

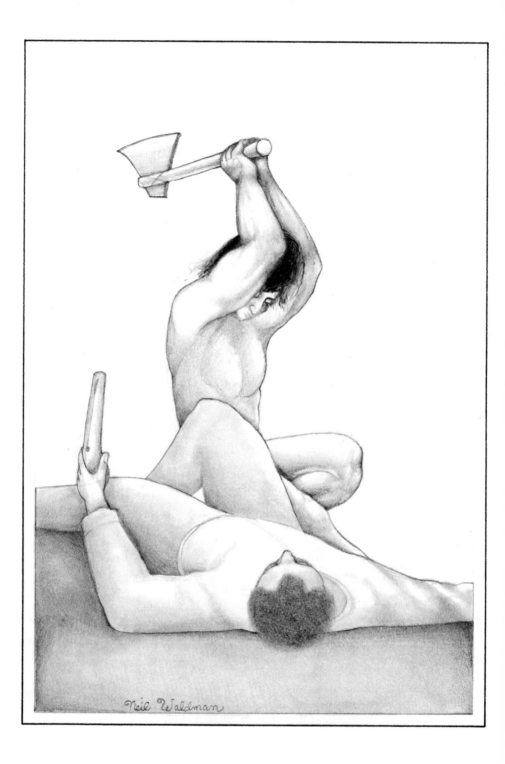

Neil Waldman

THE GHOSTS OF
FOLEY SQUARE

Little is left in Manhattan to remind visitors that the island once was inhabited by Indians and a few white traders. But today, near Foley Square, two phantom Indians from the early 1600's can still be seen walking the streets together.

They are a father and his twelve-year-old son. They walk briskly to a certain spot on one of the streets. There they stop and appear to be removing something heavy from their shoulders. Then the older one fades away and the small Indian turns and, with hands covering his face, runs back the way he came.

The tale of these two Indians begins in 1623, when the very first white settlers arrived at what is now called Manhattan. They were traders sent by the Dutch West India Company to bargain for furs with the Indians.

About a hundred men, women, and children arrived on that first ship, the *New Netherland*. They were under the leadership of a man named Cornelius Jacobsen May, who had orders to make this first Dutch colony show a profit for the businessmen who had invested in the venture. He immediately erected a few huts on the tip of the island to shelter the women and children. He also sent men to various parts of the island to prepare sites for trading posts.

A few months later more ships arrived, bringing fifty additional men with livestock, tools, furniture, and all the other things needed to make a permanent settlement.

At that time the island of Manhattan was covered with dense forests of oak, walnut, birch, and pine trees. For many months those first settlers labored at clearing small plots on which to build log huts to live in and to store the furs they obtained from the Indians.

The skins of beaver, otter, and deer were brought to the Dutchmen by bands of Indians who travelled many miles, some coming from as far north as what is now New England, and from as far south as Virginia.

The Indians gratefully accepted a few handsful of beads and trinkets in payment for the rich skins that would be worn by the royalties and aristocracies of Europe.

But not all the Dutchmen dealt in furs. Lots had been drawn as soon as the huts were erected. The few winners were to be traders; the losers were put to work clearing more areas for small farms. This was hard work. Cutting down huge trees, digging out the stumps, then plowing and sowing occupied every waking hour from dawn to darkness. These farmers envied the fur traders who had only to sit in the doorways of their huts and trade for furs with simple natives who were willing to take almost anything in exchange for skins that would bring large sums of money when sold in Holland.

One day a dissatisfied farmer went into the fur business for himself.

He had been dragging a large stump out of the ground and stopped to rest. As he sat on one of the fallen logs he saw two Indians emerge from the forest. One was fullgrown; the other was a boy. Both had large bundles of furs tied to their backs. They had trudged from what is now Connecticut to sell pelts to the white men who, they had heard, were giving fabulous treasures for the skins of animals. They were father and son.

They stopped when they saw the Dutchman and, with sign language, asked for water and food. The farmer agreed, and motioned for them to remove their packs and rest.

The farmer ran to his hut, but when he returned he brought no food or water. Instead in one hand was a gun, in the other a knife. He shot the older Indian dead, then turned and attacked the boy. The knife struck the young Indian in the face, cutting a deep gash from forehead to chin. The boy turned and ran into the forest.

The farmer buried the Indian in the hole left by the stump and hid the furs near his hut. Every week or so he'd take one skin to a trader, explaining that he had killed the animal himself and had tanned the hide. The money he obtained for the stolen furs bought tools and furniture.

The farm flourished. During the next few years he enlarged the house and married a woman who arrived from Holland in one of the many ships that sailed back and forth between the mother country and New Amsterdam.

The entire colony grew. A new governor arrived, Peter Stuyvesant, a small, tough man with a wooden leg. Stuyvesant erected buildings, laid out streets, and even built a stout wall across lower Manhattan as a shield against marauding Indians. Where that barricade was erected is now known as Wall Street.

Then one day, about ten years after he had murdered the Indian, the farmer was strolling through one of his fields of tall corn. Suddenly he was seized from behind and thrown to the ground.

Towering above him was a tall Indian who looked vaguely familiar. The farmer's mind raced, trying to recall when and where he had seen those features. Then as the red man turned his head to see if anyone was watching, the Dutchman knew. Splitting the left side of the Indian's face was a red scar from forehead to chin.

Just as the tomahawk flashed in an arc before his eyes the farmer pulled a pistol from his belt and fired upwards into the broad chest that leaned over him.

The Dutchman's widow finally sold the small farm. And eventually, as New Amsterdam slowly evolved into New York, busy streets lined with houses and stores criss-crossed the area where once rows of corn waved silken banners in the sky.

But always there were stories of the two Indians, father and son, who wandered through those streets.

They still wander there today.

Neil Waldman

THE GHOSTLY INHABITANTS OF FORT MONROE

There are dozens of old forts in the United States, and each one is home for at least one ghost. But Fort Monroe in Virginia, at the entrance to Chesapeake Bay, has the distinction of sheltering many different phantoms, apparitions, and even poltergeists.

In its nearly 400 years of existence the ancient pile of stones has witnessed more history than any other spot on the eastern seaboard.

Even before it actually became a fort its site was selected by Captain John Smith, in 1607, as a perfect place from which to guard the entrances to the James and York rivers. His helmeted and steel-breastplated ghost has often been seen stalking along the beach. He's always gazing out to sea, perhaps watching for the supply ships that never came for the tiny settlement he had christened Jamestown.

A few years after Captain Smith arrived, British settlers constructed a rough fort there. Since then it has been rebuilt, enlarged, and occupied continually by either English, French, or American armed men.

In 1781 the French fleet, under the command of Admiral de Grasse, landed marines at Old Point Comfort and captured the fort from the British soldiers who were a part of Lord Cornwallis' attack on Yorktown. It was that French fleet, aiding General Washington's troops, that finally brought about the surrender of Cornwallis on October 19, 1781, and gave the Colonies the victory they had fought so desperately to win.

Some say that the strange cries they hear around the wide moats at Fort Monroe are the spirits of British and French fighting men who gave their lives defending and attacking a plot of ground in a strange land.

However it was the Civil War that produced many of the ghosts that haunt the famous old fort.

Some nights two huge forms appear in Hampton Roads, a narrow waterway within sight of the battlements of the fort. There is the sound of exploding shells and the screams of wounded men. The hazy shapes are the two iron ships of the North and South, the Monitor and the Merrimack, fighting each other again in the darkness.

Although many unknown ghosts seem to make Fort Monroe their permanent home, other phantoms, more famous, pay it only periodic visits, as just one more stop on their rounds of places that were of great importance to them during their lifetimes. Lafayette, Lee, Lincoln, Edgar Allen Poe, John Smith, George Washington, General Grant, and Nathaniel Green, are only a few of the many famous figures that have been seen striding along the ramparts or in the rooms of the fort.

However, the most frequently seen is Jefferson Davis, President of the Confederacy, who, after the conclusion of the Civil War, was brought to the fort as a prisoner and kept in chains in a dungeon.

Jefferson Davis was a former Secretary of War during the administration of President Pierce, and a senator from Mississippi before hostilities broke out between the North and South. Probably it was the barbaric treatment of this former head of state that makes his ghost, and that of his loyal wife, Varina, haunt so many places in and around the fort.

Mrs. Davis worked long and hard to ease the condition of her husband during his imprisonment. Finally she was allowed to bring their small daughter to the fort and take up residence in several small rooms that faced the building in which her husband was shackled like an animal.

Jefferson Davis remained in the prison for two years. In 1867 he was about to be tried for treason when suddenly the United States dropped the charge, and Davis was allowed to return to his home in Mississippi.

However the time he and his family spent at Fort Monroe left deep scars on all their lives.

The windows in the rooms that had been occupied by Mrs. Davis and her daughter often rattle in their frames, especially when there is no breeze and the air is still. Wedges pounded into them don't stop the clattering. It was at these windows that Mrs. Davis used to stand and stare across the parade-ground at the window of the cell where her husband was held prisoner.

Many people who have lived in those rooms since then have seen a small, dark-haired woman standing at the windows. The phantom disappears when they approach it. At night the same small woman is often seen walking slowly around the building that held her husband. She is always alone.

Although many ghosts are literally *seen* at Fort Monroe—on the battlements, in the streets, and especially in the rooms of the buildings—there are other spirits who are never apparent, but who make their presence known by other means.

There are poltergeists, fun-loving or malicious

spirits who disrupt the normal, everyday existence of many who now live in the fort. Vases, cups and saucers are smashed or put in other places for no reason. Carpets are sometimes rolled up and stood on end. Objects are transferred from one place to another—and then put back again.

In one apartment where a captain was sleeping there was a sudden noise in the night. The captain, waking and turning on the light, saw that a picture had apparently fallen from the wall. He had heard about the poltergeists who lived in the house and was certain they had knocked down the picture. To make sure he wouldn't be further disturbed during the night he removed all the pictures from their hooks and stood them in a corner of the room. The next morning he was astonished to see that all the pictures were hanging in their places! That was one of the few times poltergeists have been known to arrange objects nicely instead of changing or destroying them.

The list of strange happenings and appearances at Fort Monroe is long and fascinating, and many tourists make the journey there in the hope of seeing something unusual. But most are disappointed.

Neil Waldman

THE WITCH
IN THE POND

What makes ghosts, phantoms and even witches appear for the first time? Strange and often terrible happenings cause these frightening apparitions to be seen. This is the story of one event that resulted in the appearance of a witch with long, flowing red hair.

Many years ago, in the early 1800's, a young minister and his wife were sent into the wilds of Pennsylvania to take the place of a very old pastor who had died.

The church was a small building next to an old log cabin, home of the old minister, and where the young pastor and his wife would live. Both church and home were on the bank of a swiftly running creek.

Not too many years before there had been many Indian raids on the small settlement. But now the settlers felt reasonably safe, and had made friends with the red men who still remained in the area.

The young minister and his wife came from one of the large eastern cities, and the untamed roughness of their new home was a shock. But they accepted their responsibilities willingly, and set to work to clean the church and their new home.

The attic was reached by a ladder. When they poked their heads through the hole in the ceiling they could see only a hodge-podge of broken furniture, rough hides of many different animals, guns, and fishing equipment.

But in the center of the loft there was one object that interested them: a battered trunk.

The light in the loft was dim so they couldn't examine it very well. But they struggled and wrestled with it until finally they dragged it into the sunlight of the yard.

It wasn't exactly a trunk, but a box of horsehide with patches of horsehair clinging to it like scabs. The minister and his wife tried to untie the leather thongs that held the box together, but the knots were very old and had become lumps as hard as stone. Finally they cut the thongs with a knife and the lid swung free.

They stood silently, staring at the contents.

Crammed inside, so many that some fell out when the lid was thrown back, were scalps, all kinds of scalps. There were patches of white hair and black hair, and on top was a piece of human skin with long auburn tresses attached to it. Half of this red hair was neatly combed, as though the girl had been killed while taking care of what must have been her pride.

The young minister and his wife stared at each other in wonder. Where had these horrible things come from? Had the old minister collected them? Had some of the Christian Indians brought them to the church as tokens of regret for their previous savagery?

But wherever they came from the duty of the young minister was plain. They would have Christian burial. He would see to it.

The cemetery of the little church, a cleared patch of ground between ancient oaks, lay across the creek. The young minister and his wife dragged the battered leather box to the bank and lifted it onto a canoe.

But when the minister pushed away from the small dock he realized he had made a mistake. The creek was swollen by a week of intermittent rain, and the currents were swifter than he had expected. But he had begun the task, and he would try to see it through.

He almost did. But midway to the other side a floating log rammed into the canoe, overturned it, and threw the box into the water. The lid burst open and spewed the scalps into the rushing currents.

As the minister clung to the overturned canoe

he saw the scalps bobbing in the water. They huddled together for a few moments, then slowly separated and floated away down stream.

A few weeks later the rumors started. The young minister began to hear tales of a beautiful woman with long red hair who lived in a pond a few miles downstream from where the scalps had fallen into the creek. She was said to help people who were in trouble.

A young Indian woman with a deformed child had gone to the pond to drown herself and her baby. But just as she was about to throw herself into the water, a woman with long red hair rose from the center of the pool and told her to go home, that in time the child's legs would be straight.

At first the Indian was frightened, but, she said, the woman was so kind and her smile so beautiful that she forgot about killing herself and ran home.

Soon many Indians from the surrounding area went to the pond to ask the red-haired girl for advice about love, wealth, and health. There were so many stories about the girl in the pond that the young minister decided to investigate.

The pond was small, a sheltered place where the creek widened on its way to join a river that led to the sea. The minister stood on the bank and studied it. It was calm there, and he could understand that some troubled people might find peace simply by staring at the serene water. But, he was sure, there must be something else.

Then he saw it.

Long tresses of red were floating in the water, just below the surface. They were so real and lovely that, even though he guessed what they were, he half expected the water to part and a beautiful girl to appear.

The legend of the witch of the pond grew stronger every year. The Indians in the area took to their hearts the story about a spirit living in the pool. The whites of the village hesitated at first, but then many of them did finally wander to the banks of the pond to ask favors of the girl with the long copper-colored hair.

The creek is polluted now, with cans, papers, and even old automobiles. The red hair long ago was carried back into the creek and finally reached the sea. But stories about the witch in the pond are still heard in that part of Pennsylvania.

There is still a strange peacefulness that seems to envelop anyone who stands on the banks of that small pool. And if you look closely, *and believe*, a girl with long red hair and a beautiful smile might appear for an instant on the surface of the calm water. Or so it is said.

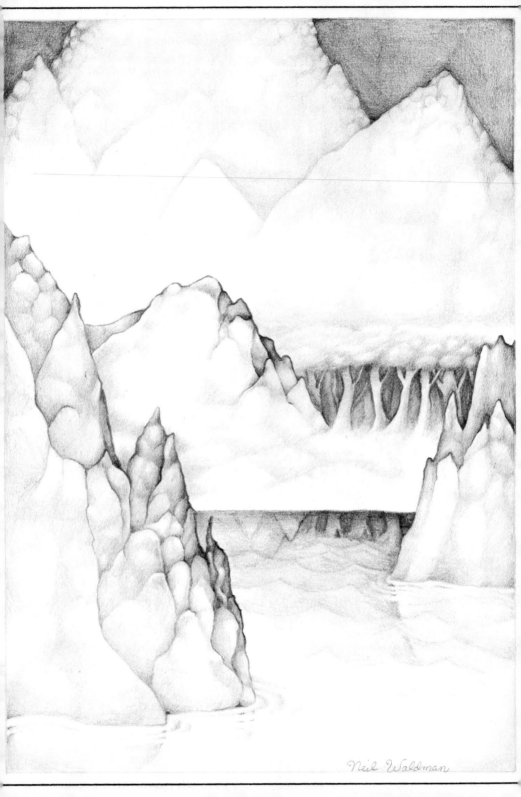

Neil Waldman

THE MYSTERY OF THE GOLD DOUBLOONS

There's a mysterious palm-shaded cove on the eastern coast of Florida. It's close to Cape Kennedy, where our space rockets blast off toward the moon. Very few people know about this lovely little lagoon, for it's off the tourist routes and difficult to find.

There's an odd stillness around this small body of water. Nothing stirs. No birds sing. No matter how violently the winds might blow from the Atlantic Ocean there's hardly a ripple on the calm water.

The water of this hidden cove is as clear as glass. Various kinds of fish swim beneath the surface, dashing in and out among the colorful coral. But, strangest of all, when standing on the bank, and looking straight down into the transparent water, gold coins, called doubloons, can be seen carelessly strewn on the sandy bottom.

But *are* these shining yellow coins really doubloons? And if they *are* real, are they protected by magic and witchcraft?

The gold pieces appear to be so close to the surface, and so easy to reach that many people have fallen on their knees on the bank and have plunged their hands into the water to pick them up. But when they open their hands the tiny doubloons have turned into seashells!

More than 350 years ago Spain's farflung colonial empire included Mexico and parts of South America. These lands were rich with gold and silver. Twice each year treasure ships left the port of Havana, where the gold pieces and silver bars were gathered, and sailed for Seville, Spain.

Other countries became jealous. England, and especially France, eyed the mounting wealth of Spain with envy. Spain placed a settlement at St. Augustine, complete with soldiers and armed ships. But the effort proved to be useless as protection for their treasure ships. French privateers (privately owned ships that stopped and robbed the treasure vessels with the permission of the French government) sailed across the ocean from Europe or from harbors in the Caribbean to rob them. By 1565 it was estimated that only half the treasure that left Havana ever reached Spanish ports. France and Spain were not at war so the privateers had to be certain they left no witnesses. Almost always they would sink the captured treasure ships and kill everyone on board.

The only answer to the problem was to send powerful warships to Havana to accompany the treasure ships across the ocean to their home port.

In 1567 a huge armada of ships left Havana to make the long journey back to Spain. Half the fleet of fifty ships were made up of vessels loaded with rare woods, skins, gold, and silver. The other half were warships carrying fighting men and cannon.

When the armada was sailing up the east coast, almost directly opposite to Cape Kennedy, a fierce hurricane swooped out of the Atlantic.

One treasure ship, the Santa Lucia, was miraculously driven by the pounding seas through a narrow inlet into the safety of the small cove.

The sailors were grateful for being saved, and immediately went ashore and gave thanks to Divine Providence. For two days and nights they feasted and prayed. On the third day they held a council to make plans.

They had a problem. With the subsiding seas the water in the narrow inlet wasn't deep enough to allow the ship to get back into the ocean. They would have to remove the cargo and in other ways make the ship light enough so that it could be pulled through the shallow water.

It took the sailors two days to unload the lumber, skins, and bags and bars of gold and silver and pile them on the beach. Then, with ropes attached to the prow of the vessel, and each man pulling with all his strength, the ship slid over the bottom of the inlet and floated free in the sea. The sailors immediately began to use their rowboats to ferry the cargo out to the ship.

They had the lumber and skins reloaded when a lookout saw a large ship bearing down on them from the north. Through a spyglass it was determined that the ship was French, and armed.

The captain of the Santa Lucia had to make up his mind at once. If he stayed where he was the French privateer would capture both the ship and the cargo. However, if he put to sea his smaller ship might outrun the larger one. In a few days he could return to the cove and reload the remainder of the cargo. He decided to up anchor and run.

All the Spanish sailors were either on board the Santa Lucia or rowing toward it in small boats, all except one. A young man, Juan Gomez Ortega, was still in the cove, checking the cargo that was left.

There was nothing to do but leave him. He would be alone in the cove for a few days, but then the ship would return.

But the ship didn't return.

French sailors captured the ship Santa Lucia,

put every Spaniard to death, removed the cargo, and sank the ship.

For many years after Ortega was abandoned on that lonely beach, Indians told tales of a mad white man who screamed and laughed as he played with heaps of gold coins, and waited for the ship that never returned. The Indians left him in peace, for to them insane people were holy. But they told the story in the narrow streets of St. Augustine, and it is entered in the old records that are kept in that ancient fort.

Some efforts were made by the Spanish government to locate the remains of the treasure ships that sank during that fierce hurricane. And a few wrecks eventually were discovered and some of the treasure brought to the surface. Then, as the years passed, there were wars and treaties and agreements, and Spain gave up most of her colonial empire. The wrecked treasure ships were forgotten.

But was the gold in that little cove ever discovered and taken back to Spain? No one really seems to know. The few who have stood on its banks and have seen the doubloons shining on the bottom say that what they thought were gold pieces might have been the reflection of the sun's rays falling through the clear water. Others claim that the doubloons are real, but are protected by a curse put on them by Ortega when he was left to die in a strange and savage land.

But all who go there agree on one thing—they have heard screams and wild laughter coming from the forest of palms trees that surround and protect that little cove with the still water. And the coins they reach for still turn into seashells in their hands.

INDEX